HIPPO **GHOST**

40p

The Face on the Wall

Carol Barton

Hippo

67

Scholastic Children's Books
Commonwealth House, 1–19 New Oxford Street,
London WC1A 1NU, UK
a division of Scholastic Ltd
London ~ New York ~ Toronto ~ Sydney ~ Auckland

First published by Scholastic Ltd, 1997

ISBN 0 590 19642 1

Typeset by TW Typesetting, Midsomer Norton, Somerset
Printed in Great Britain by Caledonian Ltd.

10 9 8 7 6 5 4 3 2 1

Chapter 1

"Aren't we nearly there yet?" Polly's voice had that whine to it that annoyed Jeremy so much.

"Don't be silly," he said. "How can we possibly be nearly there? We've only just left Clermont Ferrand, haven't we, Dad?"

Jeremy's father, who was driving the family car that towed their caravan, nodded. "That's right," he said. "I hadn't intended coming this way really, but the traffic around Lyon was so bad."

"Well, there's no hurry," said Mum soothingly. "Our time's our own. It doesn't really matter if we don't get to Marseilles until tomorrow."

"I don't see why we have to go to Marseilles." Polly pouted.

"It just seemed a good opportunity to see Susan while we're in the area," said Mum. "We haven't seen each other since school days."

"I want to get to the caravan site. I'm hot. I want a swim," Polly grumbled.

"Shut up, Polly," said Jeremy.

"Looks like that camper van in front had the same idea as us about avoiding Lyon," said Dad after a moment. "I would say they are also heading for the South of France. They were on the same ferry as us."

Jeremy was just as hot as Polly, unbearably hot as it happened, but he wasn't going to tell her that. In fact, if he was honest Jeremy hadn't been too sure about coming on this caravanning holiday in the first place.

He would have preferred to stay at home and carry on with his inventions and the experiments that he carried out in the shed at the bottom of their garden. This holiday would involve swimming and cricket and climbing and all the things that Jeremy didn't really like.

Those things would please Polly, she loved sport. Her ambition was to be a gymnast but all Jeremy wanted to do was to invent things or discover something.

His ambition was to do something really important, something that would leave its mark in history – and he couldn't see how he would achieve that on a summer holiday in France. Pulling his baseball cap down over his face he slid down in his seat and closed his eyes.

Some time later, when Jeremy came to, he realized the car had stopped.

"Are we there?" he asked, looking around. On either side of the long dusty road stretched fields of sunflowers, their glare so bright it hurt his eyes.

"You're as bad as Polly," said Mum, glancing over her shoulder. "No, we aren't there. Dad is talking to the people in that camper van. They pulled up and flashed their lights for us to stop."

"He's coming back now," said Polly a few minutes later.

"What did they want, Mike?" asked Mum.

Dad got back into the car. Jeremy noticed his father had a worried expression on his face.

"They said they've heard reports on the car radio of forest fires around Marseilles," said Dad, pulling the map out of the car pocket and spreading it over the steering wheel.

"Oh no!" said Polly. "That's all we need."

"Did they say what they were going to do?" asked Mum anxiously.

Dad was studying the map but he nodded. "They are going to head for Bordeaux," he said slowly, "but I don't really want to do that." He paused. "I think we'll head towards Toulouse."

"What's at Toulouse?" wailed Polly.

"No idea," said Jeremy, "but it looks like we're about to find out."

"What a lovely area this is," said Mum about two hours later. "Look over there," she pointed in the distance, "behind those trees — that huge house."

"Looks like a château," said Dad. "We're just coming into a small town now. Maybe we'll stop and ask if there's anywhere we can spend the night. I'm beginning to feel really weary."

Jeremy yawned and looked out of the car window as his father parked in the town square. Tall buildings surrounded the square, their shutters tightly closed against the afternoon sun. The square itself was fringed with trees, and unlike market squares at home in England, had a roof supported by thick stone pillars. Hordes of house-martins and swifts swooped and dived amongst the eaves while on the pavement a couple of thin-faced mongrels scrapped over a bone.

"These places always seem like ghost towns," said Dad as he switched off the engine. "There's not a soul in sight."

"It's the time of day," said Mum. "Look, there is one shop open over there – that little café with the tables outside. Do you want me to go, Mike? On the other hand, your French is better than mine."

"I'll go," said Dad. "It'll be nice to stretch my legs."

"I'll come with you," said Polly, unfastening her seat belt and scrambling out of the car.

Jeremy was quite happy to stay with Mum,

who opened a packet of mints and offered him one.

"There's a farmhouse just outside the town," said Dad a little later when he and Polly returned to the car. "The woman in the café said we could probably park the caravan in one of the fields."

"She was weird," said Polly. "Really weird. And all those old men sitting inside the café just stared and stared at us and never said a word, did they, Dad?"

"They probably thought you were weird," said Jeremy, turning his head to look at Polly. "And who could blame them?"

"That's a really rotten thing to say," said Polly hotly. "I'm not weird, Dad, am I?"

But Dad wasn't listening. He was driving out of the town and looking for the turning that led to the farmhouse.

"Do you think that's it?" asked Mum a little later, pointing to a dirt track at the side of the road. The track appeared to lead through a field to a cluster of buildings almost hidden by bushes and surrounded by tall thin conifers.

"I suppose it could be," said Dad doubtfully. "We'll try it."

The buildings did indeed seem to be farm buildings but as the car and caravan bumped along the track the place seemed as deserted as the town had been.

"Last Outpost again," said Mum with a laugh. Jeremy wondered what she meant and was about to ask when a black dog suddenly appeared and ran down the path towards them barking furiously.

"Well, at least that's one sign of life," said Dad.

"There's that château we saw before," said Jeremy suddenly.

"Where?" demanded Polly, bouncing up and down in her seat.

"Over there." Jeremy pointed to the left of the farm buildings across a field of yellowing grass, and tall daisies. "You can just see the roof and those pointed turret things."

"It looks like a castle to me," said Polly.

"That's just what it is, stupid," said Jeremy, pleased to have got one over on his sister.

"I'm not stupid," said Polly. "Am I, Mum?

Jeremy said I was stupid."

But Mum wasn't listening. The dog was still barking but Mum didn't even seem to be listening to that. Instead she had wound down her window and was gazing around.

"This is beautiful, Mike," she said. "What an unusual place. I do hope we can stay here. Oh, look, here comes a man now. Do you suppose he's the farmer?"

The man, dressed in old dungarees and a red checked shirt, was indeed the farmer. Dad spoke to him in French. Jeremy understood most of what Dad was saying. He was learning French at school and had done well in the end of term exams.

When the farmer replied, however, he spoke so fast that Jeremy hadn't a clue what he said.

While he was still speaking the man leaned down to peer into the back of the car as if summing them up, then he walked round the caravan, apparently inspecting it.

"Perhaps he thinks we are gipsies," giggled Polly.

"Or terrorists," said Jeremy darkly, earning a look of disapproval from his mother.

When the farmer had finally finished his inspection he walked back to Dad's side of the car and spoke again in his rapid French, all the time pointing and gesticulating at the farm buildings behind him. Then, still muttering to himself, he turned and stomped off back up the track, the noisy black dog at his heels.

"What did he say?" demanded Polly. "What did he say?"

"Can we stay, Mike?" asked Mum anxiously.

Even Jeremy found himself waiting for Dad's reply. It had suddenly become very important to him that they should be able to stay in this place. He had no idea why. It just was.

"Yes," said Dad. "We can stay. He said we've to drive through the yard to the far side. There's a clearing there apparently, where we can park up. We can buy some produce from the farm. Anything else we need we have to fetch from the town."

The clearing, bordered on one side by old farm buildings and on another by a row of thin dark conifers, was sheltered from the hot dusty winds that seemed to blow up suddenly only to die down again almost immediately.

The view from the caravan windows after Dad had parked up was of fields of misty blue lavender and beyond, a thick copse with the turrets of the château just visible above the tops of the trees.

The next hour or so was busy while Mum, helped by Polly, organized the remainder of the food they had with them, and Dad went to buy milk.

Jeremy decided to explore.

The barns and outbuildings of the farm were very old, the stonework crumbling and the huge beams supporting the roofs riddled with dry rot and woodworm. Thick red-leaved creeper grew up the sides of the buildings, almost covering the once-white walls and obscuring the windows, while in the yard clusters of old farm machinery rusted quietly away in the sun.

The farmhouse itself was vast, a two-storey building with grey painted shutters all tightly closed, its peeling walls covered by the same creeper as the barns. Apart from a few scrawny-looking chickens who pecked in the cracks between the flagstones of the yard, and the black dog who lay with its nose on its paws, eyeing Jeremy, there was no sign of any other animals.

There was, however, something very still, very quiet about the place and Jeremy, suddenly overwhelmed by an intense feeling of being watched, found himself looking over his shoulder, but the grey shutters were still tightly shut and nothing moved, not even a blade of grass.

Slowly Jeremy made his way back to the others.

Later, Mum set up their table to one side of the caravan on the grass in front of the conifers. Dad had managed to buy a French stick as well as milk and some goat's cheese. They already had tomatoes and peaches and the pâté that they had bought when they stopped in Clermont Ferrand.

By the time they had finished their meal the sun had sunk below the château but the air was still warm and they lingered around the table, all tired after their long journey.

"There's something strange about this place," said Polly suddenly and they all looked at her. She appeared very sleepy and had her elbows on the table in front of her, her chin resting on her hands.

"How do you mean, strange?" said Mum. She too looked sleepy but Jeremy thought that probably had something to do with the bottle of red wine that Dad had opened.

"I don't know," Polly replied. "I can't explain it. Just strange."

"It's certainly very peaceful, especially for a farm," agreed Mum. "Do you think it really is a working farm?"

"All the machinery seems to be rusted away," said Jeremy.

Dad chuckled. "There's a brand new tractor round the other side in a rather modern look-ing garage. And the farmer's wife told me they are expecting lots of tourists in the next few weeks."

"Does she speak English?" asked Mum.

"Very little," Dad replied.

"Do they have any children?" Polly lifted her head.

"I don't think so," said Dad.

"Oh." Polly lost interest.

"Did you ask about the château?" asked Mum.

Dad nodded and grinned. "I knew you'd want to know."

Jeremy looked up. Suddenly he too was interested in that huge old place that they could just see above the tops of the trees.

"It belongs to the de Melville family," said Dad. "They were part of the French nobility, most of whom lost their heads in the French Revolution."

Jeremy felt a tremor run through him but Polly pulled a face. "How could they lose their heads?" she asked scathingly, as if she thought it very careless that anyone could do such a thing.

"They had 'em chopped off!" Jeremy leered at her and she gave a little shriek.

"That's enough, Jeremy," said Mum firmly then, turning back to Dad, she went on, "Is the château open to the public?" Mum loved old houses and castles and that sort of thing and always visited them whenever she had the chance.

"I knew you'd want to know that as well," said Dad, "so I asked. No, the château itself isn't open to the public…"

"Oh, that's a shame." Mum was clearly disappointed. "I would love to have seen it."

"But," Dad obviously hadn't finished, "according to our hosts there is a craft fair in the château grounds tomorrow. As far as I could make out there are all sorts of activities."

"Can we go?" demanded Polly.

"Didn't you want to press on to the coast?" Mum looked at Dad.

For some reason Jeremy found himself holding his breath as he waited for his father's answer, almost as if he was willing him to say they could stay and go to the craft fair. He didn't know why he should feel that way because he wasn't usually remotely interested in that sort of thing. But suddenly it seemed very important that they should go.

"I think," said Dad at last, "we could stay here for a day or so. Maybe by then they'll have these forest fires under control." He paused. "I don't see any reason why we shouldn't go to the craft fair – it will probably be very interesting."

Jeremy gave a sigh of relief, then for some reason felt a tingle of excitement.

"Goody," said Polly sleepily.

"I think now, though," said Mum, standing up, "it's time for bed."

They began to clear up for the night, Mum and Polly taking the plates and beakers into the caravan and Dad collecting all the rubbish into a plastic bag. Jeremy sat and watched them, wondering why he felt the way he did.

"There's a rubbish bin over there by the wall of that outhouse," said Dad after a moment. "Take this over, Jeremy, there's a good chap. Make yourself useful." He handed Jeremy the plastic bag.

Slowly Jeremy got to his feet, then wandered across the yard to the rubbish bin. It was almost dark by this time but a single lamp burned high up on the corner of one of the buildings casting its glow across the yard.

Jeremy lifted the lid of the rubbish bin, stuffed the plastic bag inside, replaced the lid and had started to walk away to return to the caravan when out of the corner of his eye he caught sight of something on the wall of the building, something almost hidden by the leaves of the creeper.

He stopped, then went back, peering into the darkness.

The shadows were dense and he couldn't quite make out what it was.

Standing on tip-toe he parted the leaves.

In the light from the lamp across the yard Jeremy found himself staring into a face. A grinning, orange-coloured face that stared back at him.

Chapter 2

Jeremy's breath caught in his throat. For one moment he thought the face was real. That someone was there, hiding amongst the leaves of the red creeper, someone who had been watching them and who, now that he had been discovered, was grinning hideously at Jeremy.

The shock made him jump. Then, as he realized that the face wasn't real, but that it was made of some sort of clay or stone, he stood quite still, unable for the moment to move, staring back at it, his heart thumping uncomfortably.

"Je-re-my." It was his mother's voice calling from across the yard.

"Coming," he called. Slowly he let the leaves fall back into place, covering the face. He was beginning to feel quite silly now, that he had been so shocked by something like that.

When he got back to the others, probably because he was feeling so silly, he didn't say anything about what had happened. None of them seemed to notice if he was quieter than usual and if they did, they no doubt put it down to the fact that he too was tired.

Jeremy woke during the night. He wasn't sure what had woken him but his heart was thumping uncomfortably.

Polly was sound asleep in the other bed and all was quiet in the rest of the caravan, which suggested his parents also were asleep in their bed at the far end.

He lay on his back for a long time staring at the tiny window and the night sky bright with moonlight. He had an uneasy feeling that his waking, or possibly his dreams, had something to do with the grinning face he had seen. Which was crazy really because the face itself couldn't have been responsible for waking him, and if he had dreamt about it, the dream was over now and nothing whatsoever to be afraid of. He just wished his heart would stop thumping quite so hard.

Outside there came the cry of a bird in the darkness followed immediately by the squeal of some small animal.

Turning over, Jeremy buried his face in the pillow.

He must have gone back to sleep because the next thing he knew Polly was bouncing up and down on her bed and bright sunlight was streaming through the window.

He lay for a moment staring up at the ceiling. It seemed silly now in broad daylight that he had been so scared.

Dad had already been into the town to buy bread, croissants and fruit and when Jeremy finally tumbled down the caravan steps it was to find that Mum had set breakfast outside on the table.

"So we're all agreed on the craft fair today?" asked Dad as he poured fruit juice into beakers.

The others nodded and Mum said, "It's going to be very hot. We must all wear sun-cream and take our hats with us. I do wish the château was open to the public," she went on. "I would love to see the inside of a château."

"Never mind, I expect the crafts will be interesting," said Dad. "I understand they make some sort of clay pottery in this region. I daresay there will be some of that there."

"Is it orange?" said Jeremy suddenly.

"Is what orange?" asked Dad blankly, staring at the juice carton.

"The clay pottery," said Jeremy. He hadn't intended saying anything. Somehow it just came out.

"I've no idea," said Dad. "Why do you ask?"

"I just wondered, that's all," said Jeremy. "There's a sort of clay face over there on that wall. That's an orangey colour. I saw it last night."

"Is that why you took so long getting rid of the rubbish?" demanded Polly, eyeing him suspiciously. When Jeremy ignored her she jumped down from the table. "Show me," she said. "I want to see it."

Jeremy didn't want to show her. He wished he'd never even mentioned it. He hadn't liked the face. It had frightened him, but the last thing in the world he wanted was for his sister to suspect that.

But there was no holding Polly. She danced across the sun-drenched yard as light as thistledown in her pink cropped top and her white pedal pushers and before Jeremy even had the chance to follow her, she had found the place and was parting the leaves.

For some inexplicable reason Jeremy felt slightly sick.

"Here it is!" cried Polly, her voice shrill in the still morning air. "Come and see, Mum. It really is a face – it's a smiley face, too!"

Mum put down her coffee cup, which was still half full, and getting to her feet crossed the yard to where Polly was hopping up and down and pointing in excitement.

"Suppose I'd better go and look as well." Dad sighed and walked after Mum, leaving Jeremy to follow more slowly. He had been hoping that maybe he'd been mistaken, that he might have even imagined it, that the face hadn't really been there at all, that perhaps it had been a trick of the light, or shadows cast by the foliage. But as he drew closer he could see the splash of orange, could see the hideous grinning features and he knew that he hadn't imagined it.

"I can hardly believe it!"

As Jeremy reached the others Mum turned to look at him, and to his amazement he saw she had turned quite pale.

"Do you think you could be mistaken, Jane?" Dad was saying as he leaned forward for a better look at the face.

Mum shook her head. "No. It's exactly the same. I'd know it anywhere."

Jeremy looked in bewilderment from his mother to his father then back to the face on the wall. "What is it?" he asked, aware that once again his heart had started that curious thumping.

"This face," said Mum, staring at it, "it's identical to one on a house in the village where I lived when I was a child. I used to pass it every day; on the way to school and on the way home. I always used to look at it because it was so unusual. It fascinated me. I've never seen another one like it."

"Until now," breathed Polly.

"I don't like it," said Jeremy.

"It is a bit grotesque," agreed Dad.

"What's grotesque?" asked Polly.

"Hideous, distorted," said Dad.

"I don't think it is," said Polly, peering more closely at the face. "I quite like it."

"I wonder what the connection is," said Dad, as to Jeremy's relief they allowed the leaves to cover the face again, "between this face, I mean, and the one at home in England. Do you know who lived in the house, Jane?" he added as they all made their way back to the caravan.

"An old lady," said Mum. "The local children always said she was mad – we used to run past the house in case she came out and chased us… Oh, I've just remembered – the woman was French, how strange! Madame something or other, I don't think we knew her name."

"Well, there you are," said Dad. "That's probably the connection. I daresay she came

23

from this region – maybe she was something to do with the family who makes the faces. I don't think I'll ask the farmer, though." He laughed. "I doubt my French would run to that! Anyway, I think we'd best forget this for the time being and get ourselves organized if we're going to this craft fair."

It sounded a good idea. The trouble was Jeremy doubted he would ever forget it. He had the feeling he would remember for the rest of his life the awful moment when he had parted the leaves and that orange face on the wall had grinned at him out of the darkness.

They packed a picnic to take with them – french bread, cheese and an interesting-looking apple pastry with a glazed top that Dad had bought in the village that morning. Because the château was so close Dad decided they would walk and leave the car at the farm. It was already hot and as they trudged down the dusty farm track Jeremy could feel the warm sun on the back of his legs and on his shoulders through the thin T-shirt he was wearing.

Mum had insisted they all wore sun hats; hers was straw with a wide brim and cornflowers around the crown. Polly's hat was white cotton and she'd turned the front of the brim back and fastened it with a sunflower. Dad wore a blue pull-on hat that Mum said made him look like one of the flowerpot men, and Jeremy wore his baseball cap. He'd put it on back to front to start with but Mum had swiftly turned it round. Privately Jeremy thought it made more sense to wear it the other way as the peak would have shaded his neck from the hot sun.

In spite of the earliness of the hour there were quite a lot of people on the road to the château.

"Looks like it's quite an event for the town," said Dad as several cars swept past them.

The large wrought iron gates of the château were tightly closed but to one side a second smaller set of wooden gates were thrown wide to admit visitors to the grounds. A tent had been set up and outside, a man and a woman took the admission fees and issued tickets.

While Dad was sorting out the correct

amount of francs to pay for the tickets and Mum was trying to convert it to sterling to see how much it had cost them, Polly suddenly clutched Jeremy's arm and began hopping up and down in that embarrassing way that younger sisters have.

Jeremy's first instinct was to move away and pretend he wasn't with her. Another family were queuing behind them and the two teenage boys who were with them seemed to be giving them some very funny looks, which wasn't really surprising with the way Polly was carrying on.

"Jeremy look, you must look." Polly was gripping his arm so tightly now it was hurting.

"Look at what?" he said impatiently through the side of his mouth. He'd seen someone speak like that in a James Bond film and had known at the time it would come in useful one day.

"Back there," hissed Polly excitedly, "on the gates. It's that face again."

Jeremy paid attention then. "What face?" he swung round.

"The face ... the face on the wall back at

the farm," spluttered Polly. "Come and look, it's the same one."

"You're imagining it," said Jeremy loftily although inside, at hearing the face mentioned again, his heart had started that curious thumping.

"No, I'm not," declared Polly hotly, "come and see."

Reluctantly he followed her back to the road, where they could see the front of the iron gates that led directly to the château.

"There you are. See. I told you," cried Polly triumphantly.

Jeremy knew what he was going to see almost before he forced himself to look.

The face was there just as Polly said it was.

This one was smaller, made of metal, and set not on a wall but in the iron work of the gates – but, grinning grotesquely down at them, it was without doubt the same face.

Jeremy stared back, the queasy feeling churning in his stomach again.

"I wonder what it is?" said Polly. "Why it's here as well as at the farm?"

"Jeremy! Polly! Come on, we have the

tickets." Dad was calling them from inside the wooden gates and the other family had turned to stare.

"Come on," muttered Jeremy, "we have to go."

"But what do you think it means?" persisted Polly as he strode back to the others and she ran alongside trying to keep up.

"I don't know," he said sharply. "But I think we'd best forget it. Mum seemed quite upset about the other face. Don't say anything about this one."

"But…" Polly began to argue.

"No," said Jeremy, and she fell silent.

"Where have you been?" said Mum as they joined their parents.

"Nowhere much," said Jeremy vaguely.

"Right," said Dad, "so if you're ready, let's go in."

The crafts were displayed in a series of outbuildings, barns, tents and marquees. There were many examples of local rural craftwork, from hand-woven garments to wood carvings, from clay pottery to hand-crafted jewellery.

Mum and Polly seemed enchanted,

exclaiming at everything they saw, while Dad appeared to have become rooted to one spot in the largest barn, watching a man carving a horse's head from a huge clump of wood.

Jeremy felt restless. Not bored exactly — just restless. For some reason he didn't seem able to forget the face and found himself wondering again and again why it should be here on the gates of the château, as well as on the wall of the farmhouse, and come to that, why it should also be on the wall of that house back in England.

He wandered outside the barn and looked round. The roof of the château was just visible behind a row of tall trees. Suddenly Jeremy found himself wishing he could go inside. He didn't know why he wanted that, in fact it was most unusual, because he didn't really like visiting stately homes. Maybe, he thought, if he got closer to those trees he could get a really good look at the château.

Quietly he crossed the large courtyard, passing through little groups of people and slipping between two of the largest display tents.

To his disappointment a high stone wall ran behind the tents, obstructing any possible view of the house.

Slowly he made his way back to the others who were still in the barn. They didn't appear to have even missed him. Mum was examining a long fringed scarf and Polly was standing before a stall of puppets. Dad was still engrossed with the wood carver.

Jeremy sighed and decided to join his father.

"He's a very clever man," said Dad, throwing Jeremy only the briefest of glances as he joined him. "Just look at the way that horse's mane is appearing."

Jeremy politely agreed, then for some reason he began looking round the barn, not just at the displays of various crafts but around the walls as if he was searching for something, finally looking high up into the rafters.

And suddenly, there it was again.

His heart turned over. High on a thick, wooden beam the face grinned down at him. This time there was no holding back.

Jeremy's hand shot out and gripped his father's arm.

"Eh? What's up?" Startled, his father turned to look at him.

"Up there," whispered Jeremy, aware that the wood carver had also looked up and was watching them.

His father looked up at the beam.

"Well, I never!" he said. "It's that face again. It seems to be haunting us, doesn't it?"

"What do you think it is?" said Jeremy desperately.

"Blessed if I know," said Dad. "Maybe it's time we found out." He turned to the wood carver as if summoning the necessary French required to ask the question.

"Got a problem?" The wood carver grinned.

"Oh, I say. You're English!" Dad laughed.

"Yes," said the man. "My wife and I tour all the craft fairs. She makes puppets and dresses them in period costume. She's on the stall over there." He nodded across the barn.

"I see," said Dad, then as Jeremy tugged his arm, he went on, "we are intrigued by that face up there on the beam." As the man turned to look, he said, "You see, there's also one on the wall of the farmhouse down the road where we are staying and we wondered what it signifies."

"You'll see a few more if you stay in this area," said the man with a nod.

"Really?" said Dad.

As they waited for the explanation, Jeremy realized he was holding his breath.

"It's the de Melville family crest," said the man. "They own the château."

"Oh, I see," said Dad. "Well, that explains it. The château looks wonderful, or rather what we can see of it. My wife was hoping to see inside but we gather it isn't open to the public."

"No." The man shook his head. "Part of the gardens are open though and there's a labyrinth as well. That's well worth a visit when you've seen all the crafts."

"Yes, we'll do that," said Dad, "and thanks."

They were about to move away when the man called them back. "You may also be interested in the pageant this evening," he said. "A group from the town stage it in the château grounds. They roast a whole pig and everyone dresses up in eighteenth century costume."

"Sounds fun," said Mum a little later as they left the barns and tents of the craft fair and walked down a wide grassy pathway following signs to the gardens. Dad had just reported what the wood carver had told them.

"Can we go?" asked Polly excitedly.

"I don't see why not," said Dad, "although we don't have any costumes." He then went on to tell Mum about the de Melville family crest.

"How strange," said Mum. "About the one at home, I mean. We'll have to try and find out more when we get back."

"It explains the face on the gates," said Polly suddenly with a sly look at Jeremy.

"What gates?" said Mum.

"The gates of the château," said Polly. "The face was there on the outside, wasn't it Jeremy?"

"Yes," agreed Jeremy reluctantly. "It was."

"Really?" said Mum. "Why didn't you say?"

"Jeremy said not to," said Polly. "Didn't you, Jeremy?"

"Why did you say that, Jeremy?" said Mum, placing one arm around his shoulders as they walked on down the wide pathway and into a tunnel of cool dark trees.

"I don't know." Jeremy shrugged. He really didn't know, if the truth be known, he only knew he felt strange every time he saw one of the faces or heard one mentioned. "I thought you seemed a bit upset when you saw the one at the farm, that's all," he added.

"I don't know that I was exactly upset," said Mum slowly. "I just thought the whole thing seemed really strange, that's all – the coincidence and all that."

"Do you know something?" Dad suddenly stopped. "I think this pathway is part of that labyrinth that the wood carver was telling us about, Jeremy."

"What's a labyrinth?" asked Polly.

"Oh, for goodness' sake," said Jeremy. "Don't you know anything? It's a maze, isn't it, Dad?"

Dad nodded and Polly squealed. "People get lost in mazes," she said.

They had come out of the tall trees now and all around them were high clipped yew hedges forming dozens of pathways.

"Which way, Dad?" asked Jeremy.

"Goodness knows." Dad shrugged and laughed. "Take your pick."

They tried first one pathway, then another. Each led to a dead end. There were several other families and groups of people all exploring the labyrinth and for the next half hour or so they spent an hilarious time trying to find a way out.

In the end it was Mum who made a discovery.

"Look!" she cried, pointing down a particularly long path. "There's a clearing down there and there's something there – I'm not sure what."

"Oh, let's go and look," said Polly.

Jeremy was pleased that for the moment the face seemed to have been forgotten, then as they walked down the path and grew closer to the clearing they could see that what Mum had seen was a little building on a raised platform with steps all around it. It was made of stone columns and gilded metal and had little cherubs and angels around the domed roof.

"It looks like a temple," said Jeremy.

"I think you'll find it's what's called a folly," said Mum, climbing the steps, standing in the centre and gazing around.

"I think it's a bit creepy," said Polly. "My arms have gone all goosey."

"That's because there's no sun in here," said Dad. He glanced at his watch. "I could do with a drink. Come on, let's press on and see the gardens, then we'll make our way back to the picnic area to have lunch."

"We have to find our way out of the maze first," said Mum.

"That shouldn't be too difficult," said Dad, "there's a signpost over there." He pointed to a small white sign on the ground.

"It might be easier if it wasn't in French," said Mum with a laugh.

"What does it say?" Polly looked at Jeremy.

"It says 'This way to the gardens'," he

replied, earning a look of approval from Dad.

They walked on in silence, their feet making no sound on the soft ground. Then, just when Jeremy was beginning to think they really might be lost after all, they stepped out of the dark pathways of the labyrinth and on to a wide grassy slope that stretched before them.

To one side fountains played amongst statues, throwing their jets high into the air, the water sparkling in the bright sunlight; while to the other side, formal gardens between walkways of stately trees and clipped hedges reached almost as far as the eye could see.

"Oh!" gasped Mum.

"Wow," said Jeremy.

They moved forward, mesmerized by the unexpected splendour of the scene, then suddenly Mum turned and looked back.

"Oh, Mike!" she breathed. "Look! There's the château!"

No longer hidden by the trees it was there in all its glory, but as Jeremy gazed at it the knot of fear that seemed to have been in his stomach since the previous evening began to twist and tighten.

Chapter 3

Surrounded by terraces, balustrades and stone steps, the château was built of pink brick, its many-arched windows covered by pearly-grey shutters. It seemed to glow in the bright sunlight and for a moment even Jeremy was awestruck.

"Oh," said Mum, "it's beautiful. I wish we could see inside or even get a little closer," she added wistfully.

"Not much chance of that," said Jeremy slowly, "they've put those orange plastic cordons round to keep the public in the gardens."

"Oh well, never mind," sighed Mum. "The gardens are beautiful as well. You know,

Mike, I don't think I've ever seen anything quite like it."

Jeremy remained silent. He was inclined to agree with his mother but probably for different reasons. There was definitely something about this place that made him feel very strange but he wasn't certain he could put it into words.

They walked through the gardens with Mum exclaiming over one plant or another after every few steps.

"I'm hot." Polly was the first to complain.

"And thirsty," Jeremy added hopefully.

"We'll go back to the picnic area and have our lunch," said Dad at last.

Jeremy trailed behind the others as they made their way back up the grassy slope then, just before they entered the cool darkness of the yew trees again, something compelled him to take one last look at the château.

It was very quiet, very still. Desperately Jeremy tried to think what it was about the place that made him feel so odd. It was almost … almost as if it was imperative that he should go inside.

Yes. That was it exactly. The realization hit him with a shudder. It was as if some force was compelling him.

But why? What would he gain? And besides there was no question of him going inside. The wood carver had been quite definite about that. The château was closed to the public.

Jeremy was about to turn away to run and join the others when a sudden flash of sunlight caught his eye. He blinked, stared at the château, then blinked again. The flash had come from between two of the shutters on an upstairs window. The sun must have caught the glass – which meant those particular shutters were open.

Was someone watching him, even as he was staring at the château?

There was no way of knowing because he was too far away to tell. The thought made him shiver, and with one last look he took to his heels and ran after the others, catching them up half way through the path of yew trees.

* * *

They had almost finished lunch when Mum said she had a headache. "I expect it's the heat," she said. "It really is very hot today."

"I hope it isn't one of your migraines," said Dad. "I think we'll go back to the caravan for a siesta when we've finished lunch."

Polly groaned. "I don't want a rest," she said.

"It might be a good idea," said Mum, "then you'll be fresh for this evening."

That seemed to satisfy Polly and a little later they all trailed back to the farm. By this time they were hot, dusty and tired and even Polly was glad to collapse on to her bed.

Much to his surprise Jeremy slept and when he awoke he could hear voices outside the caravan in the yard. He glanced at Polly's bed and saw that it was empty. He listened and after a while realized it was Polly he could hear talking to Dad. It sounded as if she was pleading.

Quietly he slipped out of bed and padded outside. Polly and Dad were sitting on a bench beneath the ivy-covered wall. Trying hard not to think about what was hiding under the ivy, Jeremy walked across the yard to join them.

Polly looked up as he approached. "Mum's got one of her migraines," she said gloomily.

Jeremy threw a questioning look at his father who nodded. "'Fraid so," he said.

"Dad says we won't be able to go to the pageant." Polly's voice was almost a wail.

Jeremy felt himself stiffen.

"Keep your voice down, Polly," said Dad wearily. "You'll disturb your mother – she's only just got off to sleep."

"Is that right, Dad?" asked Jeremy.

"Is what right, son?" Dad sounded vague.

"That we won't be able to go to the pageant?" said Jeremy patiently.

"Well, I don't see how we can." Dad sighed. "You know how Mum is with these migraines. She's had one of her tablets but she'll be out of action for hours yet."

"Couldn't *we* go?" said Jeremy. Quite suddenly, for some reason, he was filled with something close to desperation at the thought that he might be prevented from going.

"Well, I don't really want to leave your

mother," said Dad with a worried frown. "Sometimes she gets very sick and I would want to be here if that should happen."

"But we could go," said Jeremy quickly. "Polly and me."

"On our own?" squeaked Polly. She was still wearing her sun hat and she peeped out at them from under the brim. The petals of the sunflower had wilted and were hanging over her forehead.

"Why not?" said Jeremy. He said it casually enough but inside, his heart had started that dreadful thumping again. "We'll be all right."

"Well, I don't know about that..." Dad began.

"It's only up the road," said Jeremy calmly, "and it sounded as if everyone in the town goes. I expect the farmer and his wife go and that wood carver will certainly be there."

"Well..." said Dad, rubbing the side of his nose.

"Can we?" demanded Polly, her eyes like saucers as the idea of their going became more of a possibility. "Oh, please, Daddy, can we? Please?"

Dad looked from one to the other of them while Jeremy waited, then at last he said, "Well, I suppose so…"

Jeremy let out his breath in a long sigh of relief. He had no idea why it was so imperative that he went back to the château, he only knew it was.

"I don't know what your mother will say…" His father was speaking again and Jeremy forced himself to listen. "But I daresay it will be all right – provided you stay together and you are back here by –" he glanced at his watch – "by nine-thirty sharp … is that clear?"

Dad still looked anxious, but Polly flung her arms round his neck and kissed his cheek. "Oh thank you. Thank you," she cried. "And we will be good. Won't we, Jeremy?"

"Well, I will be," said Jeremy. "Just make sure you are as well."

"Of course I shall." Polly pouted. "I always am. I wish we had costumes. The man said people dressed up in … in … what was it, Dad?"

"Eighteenth-century costume," said Dad.

"The pageant probably all ties in with the French Revolution theme. But I'm afraid we haven't got anything like that, neither do we have the time to make anything."

"It doesn't matter," said Jeremy sharply, suddenly afraid that Polly might change her mind, and at the same time knowing he wouldn't be allowed to go alone. "I don't suppose anyone will notice."

"No," said Dad. "I don't suppose they will."

"Everyone's in costume except us," wailed Polly as a couple of hours later she and Jeremy made their way back up the road to the château grounds. People were converging on the château from all directions. Some on foot, others by car, but it was quite true what Polly had said; all were in costume.

Some were in the finest of silks and satins with beautifully styled, powdered wigs; others were in military uniforms of scarlet or blue trimmed with gold braid and others still in peasant dress, the women and girls in low-necked dresses and the men in plain breeches and white shirts. One or two carried old-fashioned pikes, some had a patch over one eye, others wore strangely-shaped hats, and most looked quite menacing.

All, however, seemed in high spirits and called out encouragingly to Jeremy and Polly as they found themselves caught up in the throng and carried along to the gates of the château.

"You know Mum wouldn't have let us come on our own, don't you?" said Polly as she danced along beside Jeremy.

"I know," said Jeremy. "Lucky you know how to get round Dad."

Polly laughed.

"Well you'd better behave yourself, that's all," said Jeremy darkly, "because I'm not taking the blame for anything you might do."

"Don't be silly, Jeremy. What could I possibly do?" said Polly. "We're only going to a pageant."

Yes, thought Jeremy, in the grounds of a strange château, in a foreign country where everyone else speaks French. Polly found difficulty keeping out of mischief at home in

England on something as simple as a trip to the village shops. Goodness knows what might happen here.

The wrought iron gates were still tightly closed, as they had been before, and the crowd were making their way through the wooden gates by the side. Jeremy tried hard not to look at the grinning face on the gates, but he found it impossible. The face was every bit as hideous as before, the eyes staring, the grin grotesque, and he forced himself to look away.

"There's that face again," said Polly brightly.

"Yes." Jeremy nodded briefly then, changing the subject, said, "Everyone's heading for that field behind the yard and the tents. That must be where the pageant is to take place."

As they approached the field snatches of music drifted towards them along with a delicious smell of roasting bacon. A canvas-covered platform had been set up at one end of the field and before it, seats arranged in rows formed a huge semi-circle.

Tents and booths had been erected around

the edges of the field, displaying more of the crafts and wares they had seen during the day, or games and sideshows.

It reminded Jeremy of a fairground as he and Polly wandered from tent to tent. They had a go on a game like hoop-la. But it seemed to have different rules from the game they were used to at home and they lost their money immediately.

"That wasn't fair," protested Polly as Jeremy dragged her away. "I won that jug."

Next they came to the area where the pig was being roasted on a huge spit.

"Oh, poor pig," said Polly, tears filling her eyes as she realized it was a real pig.

"It's dead, silly," said Jeremy quickly, knowing the type of scene Polly was liable to make.

"It was alive once," she said, "and running around."

"So were the lamb chops you ate on the ferry," said Jeremy.

"But they weren't in the shape of a lamb," persisted Polly. "I shan't eat any," she declared firmly.

"Let's go and find a seat," said Jeremy, suddenly afraid that Polly would demand to go home and knowing that if she did, he would have no option but to take her.

As they made their way past one of the tents they caught sight of the wood carver and his wife, who waved to them.

"Enjoy yourselves," called the man.

For some reason Jeremy felt a little less uneasy after that and, finding two seats on the end of a row, they sat down to wait for the start of the pageant.

The performers, surprisingly, seemed to come from the steadily assembling throng and not as Jeremy had expected from behind the platform.

With a great deal of shouting and laughter, and to the accompaniment of flutes, drums and some stringed instruments that Jeremy didn't recognize, the players stamped and danced their way up the wooden steps to the stage.

They did seem to sort themselves out a bit then with the more finely-dressed amongst them settling themselves on to ornate chairs and sofas on the platform while the others, those dressed as peasants, fell back and watched from the wings or sat cross-legged on the grass and gazed up at the platform.

A story then seemed to begin, but because it was spoken entirely in French and because the high level of noise persisted throughout it all, Jeremy had great difficulty understanding any of it.

"What are they saying?" Beside him Polly clutched his arm.

"Haven't a clue." Jeremy shrugged. "I can only catch the odd word here and there."

Polly fidgeted and swivelled round on her chair.

"There's a cart back there with a horse pulling it," she hissed after a moment.

Jeremy looked over his shoulder and, sure enough, at the back of the field was a horse-drawn cart, the sort that farmers used. "Perhaps they're giving rides to children," he said in the forlorn hope that might hold Polly's interest.

At that moment his attention was taken again by the antics of those on the stage and he watched mesmerized as they pranced around in their silks and satins, sighing, blowing kisses to each other, eating fruit from a bowl in the centre of a gold-painted table and drinking from gold goblets encrusted with jewels.

And then at some point the mood changed, whether suddenly or gradually Jeremy wasn't quite sure. He only knew that the atmosphere on stage was different, that instead of being light-hearted and frivolous it had become tense, with the players wide-eyed and expectant.

The flute and stringed instruments had fallen silent, as had the noise and laughter in the crowd, and all that could be heard was the steady beating of a single drum.

Those performers clad in peasant dress had risen silently to their feet and had formed in two columns behind the lone drummer and as Jeremy watched they began marching around the perimeter of the field to the single steady beat.

They were a ragged bunch, in direct contrast to the richness of those on the stage.

Their leader was a tall, thin fellow with a sallow complexion dressed in a dark military-style jacket, patched trousers and a triangular-shaped hat. He carried a rifle over his shoulder while the man on his left hoisted a huge flag high into the air, furling and unfurling it around his head as he marched.

Those in the audience seemed to be waiting in anticipation for something to happen as a sense of menace appeared to descend like a cloud and settle over them all.

Uneasily Jeremy stirred in his chair. There was something about all this he didn't like. He wasn't quite sure what it was but he had the feeling it was all tied up with the de Melville family, that crest of theirs – the grinning face – and the scenes he'd once seen in an encyclopaedia of the French Revolution. His father had said something about the Revolution, about members of the nobility losing their heads. Perhaps Polly would remember what he'd said.

Jeremy turned to ask her. But the chair beside him was empty. Polly was no longer there.

Chapter 4

At first he was simply annoyed. Why couldn't she do as she was told and behave herself for once? He turned in his chair and looked over his shoulder, half expecting to see Polly at the back of the field talking to the horse or even having a ride in the cart. But although the cart had indeed moved and was making its way through the rows of chairs towards the platform, apart from the driver who was dressed in peasant's clothes, it was empty.

A sudden commotion on the platform caused Jeremy to swing round again. The players in the silks and satins had begun screaming and rushing around while the tall fellow leading the peasant band was striding up the steps.

It was really all beginning to get quite exciting and Jeremy would have liked to see what was going to happen next but he knew he really should find Polly.

With a sigh he left his chair and hurried back through the rows of spectators looking from left to right searching for Polly as he went. He remembered she was wearing a red T-shirt over flowered leggings but in spite of that amongst this colourful throng she would not have been too conspicuous.

The wood carver and his wife were standing in front of the tent which displayed their wares. They were watching the drama that was unfolding on the platform and they didn't notice Jeremy.

"Excuse me," he said, going right up to them. "Have you seen my sister?"

"Hello, there," the man smiled. "Lost the little lady, have you?"

"Yes." Jeremy nodded.

"'Fraid not," the man said, then his wife turned her head and looked at Jeremy.

"Is your sister a pretty little girl with dark hair? And was she wearing a bright red top?" she said.

"Yes." Jeremy nodded eagerly. "Yes, that's her."

"I saw her a few minutes ago," said the woman. "She was over there." She pointed to the far corner of the field.

"I see," said Jeremy. "Well, I suppose I'd better go and find her. Thanks," he added.

He was about to move away when the man suddenly spoke. "Oh look," he said, "they're loading them into the tumbrel."

Jeremy turned back to look at the platform and saw that the peasant band were forcing those dressed in the fine clothes down the steps and into the cart.

"They're off to keep their date with Madame la Guillotine," said the wood carver with a chuckle.

"Oh," said Jeremy. With one last fearful glance over his shoulder, uncertain now that he actually wanted to see any more, he fled.

When he reached the far corner of the field

he saw there was an opening in the hedge. With one last look around to satisfy himself there was no sign of Polly he plunged forward and through the gap.

He was on a wide grassy pathway, cool and quite dim now that the evening shadows had started to lengthen.

He stopped and looked around him. All was silent and very, very still.

"Polly," he called uncertainly. No one answered and everything remained as still as before.

Jeremy felt a sudden stab of alarm. Supposing something had happened to Polly. It was true she could be really irritating and sometimes drove him quite mad but she was his sister, and he couldn't bear the idea that she might have come to any harm. And quite apart from that the thought of having to go back to the farmhouse and telling his parents that he had lost her was quite horrendous.

Suddenly he felt really annoyed. Where was Polly? She'd been told she had to behave herself and now here she was wandering off on her own. She really was the absolute limit.

Jeremy wished he hadn't come, wished he hadn't said he'd look after her.

He hurried forward down the pathway, which twisted and turned in several directions.

Then he stopped again and called, much louder.

"Polly! Polly!"

A further moment of silence was this time followed by the most fearful crashing and whirring sound. Jeremy spun round, almost startled out of his wits, and was just in time to see a bird, possibly a pigeon, rise out of the bushes and flap indignantly away.

He felt weak with relief but at the same time a little foolish that he should have been so frightened by a bird. Gritting his teeth he started forward again, aware that his heart was thumping uncomfortably. It reminded him of how it had felt before when he'd seen that awful grinning face.

"Polly!" he shouted. He was angry now, angry with Polly, but angry also because he'd been so frightened. "Where are you?" Still there was no reply but as he turned yet another corner, ahead of him he thought he caught a flash of red, the bright scarlet red of Polly's T-shirt.

She was there. Ahead of him. Playing games with him.

He started off in hot pursuit, his feet pounding on a carpet of soft peaty soil.

Panting, he rounded the corner expecting to see Polly laughing at him, dancing away from him in that maddening way she had.

Instead he faced a dead end – a solid hedge of closely packed yew.

And suddenly, quite suddenly he knew where he was. He was in the labyrinth. His stomach churned with fear and he turned again and crashed wildly back the way he had come only to find that also was a dead end. But it couldn't be. That surely was the way he'd come?

Twisting again, swallowing a catch in his throat that if it were released might have sounded suspiciously like a sob, he ducked and searched frantically along the yew hedge until he found another opening.

This time to his relief a long path stretched before him. A gloomy path dark with foliage and thick with shadows.

He began to run, his feet pounding on the ground, then as he reached the end and turned, yet another path was there, equally as long. But this time at the very end the last rays of the evening sun filtered through the trees and there in the light he saw the figure of a girl.

But it was not Polly. This girl wore a long blue dress and her hair was fair and hung down her back almost reaching her waist. She turned and looked at Jeremy.

"Hello?" he called uncertainly.

The girl stared at him through the long tunnel of trees then she laughed and danced away out of the patch of sunlight.

"Oh, no, don't go!" Jeremy shouted. "Wait, please."

He ran forward gasping and panting but when he reached the patch of sunlight there was no sign of the girl. He spun round. Three pathways led from the clearing. He didn't know which to choose. One was even darker than the others, the greens of the tunnel of trees and hedges almost black; another, although lighter, looked as if it might be a dead end.

Jeremy picked the third and knew he had chosen correctly when on reaching the end he caught a brief glimpse of the girl's blue dress ahead of him and heard the sound of laughter. Polly's laughter.

"Polly!" He shouted but once again he was greeted with silence. The laughter had seemed to come from just the other side of the hedge which probably meant Polly and the girl in the blue dress were on a pathway that ran parallel to the one he was in. If he was very quick he could catch them.

Taking a deep breath he plunged forward, sped to the end of the path and turned, expecting to catch his sister red-handed. Instead he was faced with another dead end. In dismay he stared at the hedge which towered above him. Turning, he attempted to retrace his footsteps, only to find the opening he could have sworn he'd just passed through was blocked.

He stopped and frantically looked around him. Suddenly he had the weirdest sensation that the dark hedges were growing closer, edging forward, hemming him in completely.

"Je-re-my. Je-re-my." The voice was high pitched, lilting, the accent decidedly French.

He spun round again then realized that there was a pathway, one that ran to the left, one he had missed before. He was about to charge headlong forward when he realized he could see something at the end of the path. He stopped again and peered through the gloom.

The object looked solid, a structure of some kind. He hurried forward and as he grew closer he realized it was the folly they'd seen that afternoon.

"Thank goodness for that," he muttered. He felt he could get his bearings from there. The grassy slope. The gardens. The château itself. And then it would be a simple matter to get to the road.

All Jeremy wanted at that moment was to find Polly then to go back to the farmhouse. He had no thoughts now of returning to the pageant. He couldn't really care less what had happened to the people in the cart.

The folly was in yet another clearing. Again there were less shadows, but as Jeremy approached he jumped as a figure suddenly stepped out from behind one of the columns.

This time the figure was of a boy. A boy a little older than Jeremy with hair so fair it looked almost silvery, and very pale skin, and who was wearing the same type of costume as the players on the platform; a purple satin shirt, pale grey trousers that ended at his knees and shiny black shoes with silver buckles.

"Who are you?" Jeremy eyed the boy warily.

"Philippe de Melville," said the boy.

"Oh," said Jeremy. "I'm Jeremy. Jeremy Browne."

"I know." The boy replied in French.

"I'm looking for my sister, Polly." In his haste Jeremy spoke half in French and half in English. "Do you know where she is?" He looked round as he spoke at the dark pathways that led from the clearing in many different directions.

The boy came down the steps then, lifting his head and raising one hand to the side of his mouth he called a single name. "Hélène … Hélène…"

Jeremy listened, but still there was only silence from the depths of the labyrinth.

"Hélène!" The boy called again, louder this time, and a moment later the sound of stifled giggles could be heard very close by.

The boy strolled forward across the clearing and peered round a tree. There was the sound of further laughter, then to Jeremy's relief the girl in the blue dress stepped out into the clearing leading Polly by the hand.

"Thank goodness for that," said Jeremy quite crossly. "Wherever have you been?"

"Playing hide and seek," said Polly defiantly. "With my new friends," she added, flashing a quick glance at the other two.

"You might have told me," grumbled Jeremy. "I was really worried. I thought something might have happened to you."

"Don't be silly." Polly laughed. "What could possibly have happened to me? Honestly, Jeremy, at times you're worse than Mum."

"I'm supposed to be looking after you…"

"I can look after myself," retorted Polly.

"You shouldn't have wandered off."

"If I hadn't I wouldn't have met Hélène and Philippe." Polly pouted, then, more brightly and with another glance at her new friends, she said, "They live in the château."

Jeremy stiffened.

"They were about to take me inside," said Polly.

Inside. Go inside the château? Jeremy's heart began that thumping again.

"We don't really have time for that," he said, "we have to get back, Polly. It's nearly time. You know what Dad said. Perhaps we could come back tomorrow," he added when he saw Polly's rebellious expression.

Philippe and Hélène had been staring at them as they had been speaking, watching closely as if trying to follow the gist of what they were saying. Jeremy turned to them and in rather halting French said, "Could we come and see you … tomorrow…?"

The boy shook his head and spoke rapidly.

"Oh, what did he say?" demanded Polly impatiently.

"He said," Jeremy replied slowly, "that he

and his family are going to Marseilles tomorrow … to join … I think he said … to join someone. Friends, I think."

"They must be going to Marseilles on holiday," cried Polly, clasping her hands. "Oh, Jeremy, do you think they know about the forest fires? Maybe they haven't heard. You must tell them. Warn them."

"Oh dear," said Jeremy, wondering just how far his French would go. "Well, I'll try. We are on holiday," he began in French as the boy and his sister listened attentively. "We were going to Marseilles first … but then … we heard about… Polly, what's the French for fire?" he asked desperately.

Polly's eyes widened and she shrugged helplessly. "I don't know," she said.

"Er… Danger," said Jeremy at last. "Danger … do you understand?"

Philippe still seemed bemused and shook his head.

"Danger … Marseilles," said Jeremy again, more urgently this time.

Polly nodded excitedly. "Yes," she added, "Danger … you mustn't go there."

"Ah, *dangereux*!" At last a gleam of understanding entered Philippe's eyes then he spoke to Hélène but so rapidly that Jeremy was hardly able to follow a word. Then he turned to Jeremy and more slowly, he spoke again.

"Oh, what is he saying? What is he saying?" Polly clutched Jeremy's arm and began dancing up and down.

Jeremy frowned. "He said he wants us to go with him and tell his ... tell his father about ... about Marseilles..." he said.

"Can we? Can we?" pleaded Polly.

"We shouldn't really," said Jeremy. "We don't have the time."

"It won't take long," protested Polly. "And just think ... just think how you'd feel if they went to Marseilles and were all burned to death."

"Oh, for goodness' sake, Polly," said Jeremy crossly. "I'm sure that's not likely to happen and besides, I don't see that I can tell Philippe's father any more than he can."

"But his father might listen to you," said Polly. "Parents are like that, aren't they?

They'll listen to other people and believe what they say, whereas you could have told them the same thing and they would never have believed you in a million years."

"Yeah…" Slowly Jeremy was forced to agree. "I guess…"

"And another thing," said Polly. "We'll be able to tell Mum we've been inside the château … we'll be able to tell her all about it. They'll forget about us being late."

Jeremy was far from convinced about that but by this time Polly and Hélène had hold of each of his hands and were drawing him forward, following Philippe, who had started off down one of the pathways.

It seemed in no time at all they had left the dark passages of the labyrinth behind them and as they reached the long grassy slope that led to the gardens they began to run.

The sun had set by now, leaving only a deep, crimson glow in the darkening sky. When they reached the end of the slope they stopped and turned towards the château and it was then that Jeremy's heart almost stopped.

Chapter 5

The château was a blaze of lights. Its shutters, so tightly closed before, were now thrown wide. Figures moved about in the rooms and on the terrace, and as they approached, light tinkling music floated across the gardens towards them.

"Oh," Polly gasped. "Isn't it lovely! It looks so different now."

The girl, Hélène, turned and laughed. With her golden hair, her blue eyes and her pink and white skin she reminded Jeremy of one of Polly's dolls. The dolls she never played with, the dolls that sat on a shelf at home in her bedroom.

Lost for words he allowed the girl to lead

him through the gardens. Normally the last thing Jeremy would allow was for a girl to hold his hand. But somehow this wasn't quite normal. Even the scent of flowers in the garden was almost overpowering. Mum had admired the gardens that afternoon, had even commented on the scent, but surely it hadn't been this strong?

It was a bit like the time Grandma had come to stay. Jeremy had to share Polly's room and Grandma had been in his room where she'd broken a bottle of perfume. The smell had been there for weeks. Jeremy shuddered at the memory, then he had no further time even to think of such things as Philippe ran ahead of them up the steps to the terrace where he paused, then looked back and beckoned for them to join him.

As they reached the top of the steps, with a sudden uncomfortable jolt, Jeremy found himself staring at another of those wretched faces. This time it was in stone, grey stone, and it was set into one of the balustrades. He didn't want to look at it, so he quickly put his head down and hurried on.

When they reached the terrace he came to the conclusion that the pageant must have moved from the field to the château where the players were now enjoying a party. There was, however, no sign of those in peasant costume, only those in the sumptuous dress of the wealthy. Both men and women, in curled powdered wigs, dressed in silk, satin or velvet with trimmings of gold and lace, white stockings and buckled shoes, drifted up and down the terrace. Some drank from jewelled goblets, the women playing with feathered fans and talking in shrill, high-pitched voices, the men bowing or calling to each other.

One or two in the gathering called out to the children as they passed through their midst and Philippe would pause and bow, or Hélène would smile and wave.

At last they reached the château itself and entered by way of the huge double doors that opened directly on to the terrace.

The room they entered was enormous with marble columns and floor, its walls covered with portraits and tapestries. The furniture was painted gold with red velvet upholstery and from the high ceilings hung crystal chandeliers set with hundreds of lighted candles.

And now there was no escaping the grinning face, for it was everywhere; on the mouldings on the walls, set into the frames of portraits, on the mantel above the fireplace and carved into the backs of chairs.

Jeremy shuddered, then glanced at Polly as they followed Philippe and Hélène through the room. Her mouth was slightly open, her eyes like saucers, as she gazed about her in astonishment.

Philippe led the way into another room which, although much smaller, was no less sumptuously furnished.

"Please," he said in French, "wait here. We will ask our father to come and talk to you."

As Philippe walked across the room it occurred to Jeremy that his hair was tied back and secured with a velvet bow. There was a boy at home who had come to school with his hair in a pony-tail and Jeremy's headmaster had sent him straight home to get it cut. Maybe, thought Jeremy, headmasters in

France weren't quite so strict.

"I wish Mum could see all this," said Polly as the doors closed behind Philippe and Hélène.

"Yes," agreed Jeremy, "she would love it. But I hope they won't be too long," he added anxiously. "We are going to be awfully late – it was a quarter past nine when I was talking to the wood carver. I saw his watch."

Polly crossed the room and sat down on a green brocade sofa.

"I 'spect they have a lot of fancy dress parties," she said, looking round the room.

"Or pageants," said Jeremy.

"Yes, or pageants," agreed Polly. They fell silent then while they waited for Philippe and Hélène to return with their father.

There was a window on the far wall, its shutters slightly open to the darkening night sky, and after they had sat in silence for some considerable time Jeremy thought he heard a distant rumble of thunder.

He threw Polly a sharp glance. He knew she hated thunder. Luckily she didn't seem to have heard. He hoped the storm would stay in the distance, at least until they had the chance to get back to the farmhouse.

"I wonder," said Polly a little later, "if they don't go to Marseilles, I wonder if we could come back tomorrow and play."

"I don't know." Jeremy shrugged. He wasn't sure how he felt about that – whether he wanted to come back here or not – but even as he considered it a sudden flash of lightning illuminated the room. It was followed almost instantly by a terrific clap of thunder. Polly screamed and jumped to her feet.

Jeremy darted to the window and looked out into the darkness. He couldn't see anything, but outside he could hear the first drops of rain as they began to fall on the leaves of a bush near the window. He tried to lean out of the window but the sill was too high. Looking down to see if there was anything he could stand on his eye fell on yet another of the faces. This time it was moulded in the plaster around the window frame.

It grinned back at Jeremy just as another flash of lightning lit the room.

"Come on," he said sharply, "we're going." Turning, he grabbed Polly by the hand, dragged her across the room and tugged open the door.

Outside in the large room people were dashing to and fro as they poured back into the house from the terrace and grounds, all intent on getting inside away from the storm.

There was no sign of either Philippe or Hélène.

Fighting their way through the crowd Jeremy and Polly forced their way outside on to the now deserted terrace.

Thunder still rumbled around them but the rain seemed to be confined to a few large thunder drops that plopped on to the ground.

"Come on," said Jeremy, "we'll make a run for it. If we hurry we can get home before it comes on to rain too hard."

"But which way do we go?" gasped Polly.

They paused in their flight looking from right to left. "We don't want to go back into the gardens," said Jeremy, "otherwise we'll end up in the labyrinth again." The thought of the labyrinth in a storm was quite

74

terrifying. "Come on," he said, "we'll go this way. There must be another way back to the road."

Dragging Polly behind him he took off across the terrace. A second later there came another flash of lightning followed by a crack of thunder so loud that it seemed to split the sky in two. Behind them in the château a woman screamed, then as they rushed headlong around the side of the building the raindrops grew heavier and they were plunged into sudden darkness.

"Come on, Polly, run," cried Jeremy. Already he could feel his shirt sticking to his back and rain running down his face.

They ran on through the darkness, the great walls of the château towering above them on one side and on the other what seemed to be an outer stone wall above which, briefly visible in the flashes from the lightning, was the dense blackness of trees.

Gasping and sobbing and soaked almost to the skin they rounded a corner of the building and found themselves in what seemed to be a dimly lighted courtyard. Jeremy stopped dead and Polly crashed into him.

"W-w-where ... are ... are ... w-we?" she stuttered, her teeth chattering with fear and cold.

"I don't know." Jeremy peered around.

Then from the darkness he heard the faint whinny of a horse followed by the clinking sound of a bridle.

"It must be that horse and cart they were using in the pageant," whispered Polly. "It's over there through that archway."

They crept forward, their wet hair plastered to their heads. Then, as they peered through the archway, they stopped and stared in disbelief.

Instead of the humble cart pulled by the rather elderly horse, on the flagstones in front of the main entrance of the château was a carriage and four white horses.

"It looks like Cinderella's coach," said Polly.

Rain dripped from the horses' manes as they waited patiently, then even as Jeremy and Polly watched men began carrying boxes from the house to the coach and the horses began stamping and snorting, anxious now to be away.

"What d–do you th–think it's all about?" stammered Polly.

"I don't know." Jeremy shook his head. "But we have to find a way out. It must be around here ... that coach came in some-where…"

Wildly he looked around, then Polly grabbed his arm.

"Look!" she cried, pointing. "Down there … isn't that those big gates we saw?"

Jeremy peered through the darkness and at the end of what looked to be a drive he could just make out the outline of the wrought iron gates.

"Come on…" he cried, grasping Polly's hand again. Together they ran through the pouring rain down the drive towards the gates.

"They're locked!" gasped Polly as they reached the gates and almost flung them-selves against the railings.

In desperation they rattled the bars, but the gates remained firmly shut.

"What shall we do, Jeremy?" Polly's voice was almost a sob now.

"We have to find another way out," said Jeremy. Still holding Polly's hand tightly he began to inch his way along the wall. It was still raining very hard, his trainers were squelching water and he was beginning to feel quite cold. Suddenly, to his relief, his fingers found a break in the stonework of the wall.

"There's a door here," he muttered.

"Is it locked?" gasped Polly.

The handle was a metal ring. Grasping it, Jeremy turned it sharply, pushed, then when nothing happened, pulled it. The door swung inwards and they scrambled through. Pausing only long enough to shut the door behind them, they began to run.

A car suddenly passed them and inside Jeremy caught sight of a band of revellers in peasant costume. They all shouted and waved as they roared past. Jeremy and Polly sped on down the road, leaving the château behind them, then almost before they knew it they were at the dirt track that led to the farm house and their father was there strolling down the lane to meet them.

"We're sorry we're late," said Jeremy breathlessly as they ran up to him.

"You're not late." Dad looked at his watch. "It's not quite half past nine yet. I was going to walk up to the château to meet you."

Jeremy stared at him. Not late? What on earth was he talking about. Of course they were late. They had to be late. Why, it had been nine-fifteen when he had been talking to the wood carver and that had been ages ago. They had been waiting in that room for what must have been at least half an hour, then there had been all that business in the labyrinth.

"I was scared of the thunder," said Polly.

"Thunder?" said Dad. "What thunder? There hasn't been any thunder."

"But we're all wet..." Polly began then, looking down at herself, she trailed off into silence.

Jeremy stared at her in disbelief. Where only moments ago she had been soaked to the skin, her red T-shirt sticking to her, her dark hair plastered to her head and the water running down her face in rivulets, now she was quite dry.

Quickly he looked down at his own clothes and his trainers. They too were bone dry.

They walked alongside their father up the dirt track to the farm house. Jeremy felt too stunned to say anything and even Polly seemed subdued into silence.

It wasn't until they were half way up the track that Jeremy realized that the sky was still crimson in the west and the shadows had only just begun to lengthen into dusk. When they had been in the château grounds it had been quite dark.

"I was wet," said Polly later as they lay in their beds in the darkness.

"I know," said Jeremy. "So was I."

They were silent for a while then Polly said, "I feel bad now about rushing off like that."

"We had to really…"

"It was all my fault. If it hadn't been for the thunder… And now Dad says there wasn't any thunder."

"Well, there was," said Jeremy fiercely, "we

both heard it." He was silent again as they listened to the crickets outside the caravan, then slowly he said, "I know what you mean though about feeling bad."

"Do you?" said Polly quickly.

"Yes. I feel bad too. They asked us to wait while they fetched their father. Goodness knows what they must have thought when they got back and found we'd gone."

He sighed. "Well, there isn't a lot we can do about it now so I suppose we'd better go to sleep. Good night, Polly," he added firmly. Suddenly he wanted quiet so that he could think about all that had happened and he couldn't do that with Polly chattering.

"'Night, Jeremy." Polly turned over and burrowed into her pillow.

Now it was quiet. Now he could think. On the other hand he didn't really know where to start. The whole thing had been so odd, so bizarre, and yet he couldn't quite put his finger on the time it had all changed and become so strange and unreal.

Had it been the pageant? That had been different, different from anything Jeremy had ever seen before – but not particularly odd.

So had it been the game of hide and seek in the labyrinth? He had been frightened then, it was true, but surely that had only been because he was afraid that something may have happened to Polly and not for any other reason.

Then there had been Philippe and Hélène, what of them? They too had been different, but they were French after all, so some things would automatically seem different. So maybe the château…?

"Jeremy?" Polly's voice came through the darkness.

"Yes, Polly?" he sighed.

"It was weird, wasn't it?"

"What was weird?"

"All of it," she said in a small voice.

"No," he said bravely, "I don't really think it was weird. Just different, that's all."

"Well, I think it was weird," said Polly. "And I feel scared."

"Well, there's definitely nothing to be scared of," said Jeremy. "I can tell you that now, so you might as well go to sleep."

"All right," said Polly after a while. " 'Night, Jeremy."

"Good night, Polly."

He wasn't scared. Of course he wasn't. At least, certainly not about the events of the evening. The only thing that scared Jeremy was that face and there had been rather too many of those for comfort in the château.

Yes, that was it, he told himself firmly. That was the only odd, strange thing about it all, the way that horrible face kept appearing when he was least expecting it.

Chapter 6

Mum's migraine was a little better the following morning but she was still not feeling quite right so Dad took her a cup of tea in bed then joined Jeremy and Polly for breakfast.

"I've decided," he said, "that we'll stay here another day, then if Mum is feeling better tomorrow we're going to move on. I've been listening to the radio again and they say that those fires are practically out of control around Marseilles. They've even started evacuating people, so your mother and I have agreed that we're going to give Marseilles a miss altogether and head straight for the caravan site further along the coast well away from the fires."

"What about Mum's school friend?" asked Polly.

"Well, she didn't know we were coming, so she won't be disappointed," said Dad. "Mum and I just don't think it's worth taking the risk." They were sitting at the table outside the caravan in the morning sunshine and as he finished speaking, Dad stood up. "I'll just go and see if your mother wants any more tea," he said.

As he disappeared inside the caravan Jeremy and Polly looked at each other.

"I think we should go back," said Polly firmly.

"I don't know…" Jeremy began hesitantly.

"You heard what Dad said," she went on, "the fires are out of control. We have to make sure they don't go."

"I expect their father will have heard the news on their radio," said Jeremy, but he knew he sounded far from convincing.

"But he may not," said Polly firmly. "I don't think we should take the chance."

"Do you think Dad will let us go back?"

"Yes." Polly paused, then added: "At least I

think he would if we told him."

"Told him what?" Jeremy looked faintly alarmed. He couldn't imagine trying to explain what had happened the night before.

"Leave it to me," said Polly as their father suddenly reappeared in the doorway of the caravan. "I'll tell him…"

"I'm not sure what you two are going to do," said Dad. He had an anxious expression on his face. "Mum really isn't up to going anywhere today."

"That's all right," replied Polly calmly. "Actually we have something to do."

"You do?" Dad frowned but he seemed relieved.

"Yes," said Polly then, with a quick glance at Jeremy, who remained silent, she carried on, "You see, last night when we went to the pageant, we met the children who live in the château."

"Really?" Dad looked surprised. "I got the impression no one lived there."

"Oh, but they do," said Polly. "Two children. Philippe who was about twelve or thirteen and Hélène who was a bit younger than me – isn't that right, Jeremy?"

Jeremy nodded.

"We played a game with them in the labyrinth then they invited us inside…"

"You went inside the château?" Dad was staring at them in open amazement now.

"Oh yes," said Polly. "We didn't think you'd mind because they wanted us to meet their parents. They said they were going to Marseilles today as well and we told them about the danger, you know, because of the fires."

Jeremy decided he should add something to this. "They wanted us to tell their parents what we'd heard," he said.

"And did you?" asked Dad.

"No," Jeremy shook his head. "It was getting late," he said, "and we thought we should be getting home." He didn't mention the storm again. That seemed pointless somehow, especially as Dad hadn't seemed aware that there had been a storm in the first place.

"So what do you want to do today?" said Dad, scratching his head.

"We thought we'd go back and see Philippe and Hélène," said Polly. "And make sure they're really not going to go to Marseilles. That's all right isn't it, Dad, if we do that?"

"Well," said Dad slowly. "I suppose it is…"

"Goody." Polly scrambled out from behind the table. "I'll get my sun hat."

"You mean you're going now? Right away?" Dad still looked bemused.

"I think we'd better," said Jeremy solemnly. "Just in case they'd intended making an early start."

"Right…" said Dad slowly then, as Jeremy also stood up and turned to go back inside the caravan to get his cap, he called after them. "What was it like?" he said.

"What was what like?" Jeremy paused and looked back.

"The inside of the château?"

"Like a palace…" said Jeremy.

"Weird," said Polly, then hastily, in case Dad changed his mind about letting them go back, she added, "but yes, like a palace. Just like a palace really."

* * *

88

"It's going to be hot again," said Polly as they trudged up the road to the château.

Jeremy nodded. "It feels as if there could be another storm brewing."

"Oh, don't say that," said Polly. "That's all we need."

Jeremy didn't reply. He was beginning to feel very apprehensive and was just wondering whether this had been such a good idea after all. Everything seemed very quiet that morning with only the odd car that passed them on the road, not like the evening before when the road had been packed with all those people in costume on their way to the pageant.

When at last they reached the large wrought iron gates Jeremy wasn't really surprised to see they were shut and this time he noticed a thick chain was wound round the bars with a heavy padlock on it. Had that been there before? He couldn't really remember. The face was there, of course. But then that would be. No chance of that disappearing, he thought grimly, as he gazed back at the grinning features.

"There's someone there," Polly hissed suddenly.

"Where?" Jeremy turned and found Polly had wandered a little way off and was peering over the wooden gates where they had entered the grounds the previous day.

"Down there." As Jeremy joined her she pointed down the pathway to the figure of a man who seemed to be clearing up rubbish and placing it in a large sack. "Do you think he'll let us in?"

"Don't know," Jeremy replied. "I suppose we can ask. I say," he called, "excuse me…"

The man took no notice and carried on with what he was doing. Polly suddenly giggled.

"I don't know what's so funny," said Jeremy.

"He's probably French," said Polly. "He wouldn't understand you."

"Oh," said Jeremy. "I forgot." He took a deep breath. "Excusez-moi?" he called again, much louder this time, but the man didn't as much as look up. He continued with his work, moving further and further away from them down the pathway that led through the yard to the meadow and the labyrinth.

"Perhaps he's deaf," said Polly gloomily.

"Well, I can't do much about that," said Jeremy. "And really when you think about it, we don't want to go in this way, do we? I suggest we go back to the main entrance, follow the wall round and see if we can find that little door we came through last night."

"What will we do if that's locked as well?" asked Polly breathlessly.

"I don't know. We'll worry about that if it happens," said Jeremy.

The door seemed further away from the main gates than it had the night before but at last they found it. Set deeply into the stone wall it looked smaller than it had before and was partly hidden by the branches of a large bush.

"Is it locked? Is it locked?" Polly began to jump up and down in excitement as Jeremy took hold of the large ring handle and turned it.

The handle was very rusty and large flakes came off in his hands. That was strange, he hadn't noticed that before. He pushed and for one moment as the door refused to budge, he thought it was indeed locked, then quite suddenly it moved – only an inch or so, but it definitely moved.

"It's very stiff," he said over his shoulder to Polly, then as he pushed even harder and the door yielded a little more, he went on, "It feels as if there's something behind it. Come on, Polly, you'll have to help me shift it."

Together they strained and shoved until at last they managed to push the door far enough open for them to squeeze through. A large pile of rubbish was wedged against the door; dead leaves and branches along with a couple of empty plastic containers and some old newspapers.

"I don't remember all that being there last night," said Polly, eyeing it suspiciously.

"Neither do I," said Jeremy, "but you have to admit we were in a bit of a hurry last night and it was very dark."

"Yes," Polly agreed then, after a moment's hesitation, she added, "that was something else, wasn't it, Jeremy?"

"What?" he said, knowing what she was going to say.

"Well, when we were in the meadow watching the pageant it was still daylight, then when we were at the château it was dark, but then ... later when we met Dad the sun was still only just setting... What do you think it was all about, Jeremy?"

"I don't know, Polly," he said. "I really don't. I wish I did." They stared at each other for a long moment then with a little shrug Jeremy turned towards the path to the driveway that led up to the château. "Come on," he said, "now that we've got inside we'd best get on with what we came to do."

Once again his heart had started that dreadful pounding but it had happened so often now that in some strange way Jeremy was almost getting used to it.

The drive seemed in a very bad state of repair with huge potholes and knee-high weeds lining the edges and pushing up through the gravel. At the end of the drive they passed through the archway and found themselves on the huge forecourt before the pink stone walls of the château.

Jeremy found himself looking for the coach

and horses that had been at the main entrance the night before, but today the forecourt was empty, the massive front doors were tightly closed and the grey shutters covered the many windows. Two of the upstairs windows even had strips of wood nailed across them where the shutters were missing.

"It doesn't look as if there's anyone at home," said Jeremy, standing back and looking up at the building.

"Oh dear," said Polly. "Do you think we're too late? Do you think they've already left for Marseilles?"

"I don't know." Jeremy slowly shook his head. "I'm not sure what to think. But I guess there's only one way to find out."

Boldly he strode up the steps to the front door where he grasped the chain of a large bell that hung on the wall and pulled it. A loud clanging filled the air, echoing around the forecourt and bouncing back off the walls.

But when the last echo died away there was only silence. Silence inside the great château, and silence outside.

"There's no one here," said Jeremy after a

moment, frowning as he caught sight of rubbish that had blown into the alcove around the front door. "We might as well go back."

"No. Not yet," said Polly quickly. "Let's go round to the terrace, maybe we will be able to see inside from there."

Silently they crept around the outside of the great château, retracing their footsteps of the night before when they had fled from the storm.

To their disappointment the terrace was deserted.

The stonework of the balustrades appeared crumbling now and in poor repair, and where they had hoped to see inside, to that huge room where the party had been, again grey shutters obscured the windows, their paint-work chipped and peeling.

"It almost looks derelict," said Jeremy, "as if no one has lived here for a very long time."

"Which is stupid," said Polly, "because it was only last night that we saw them. They were all here … weren't they, Jeremy?"

"Yes…" Jeremy nodded, but absent-mindedly, for he was trying to peer through a chink in the shutters.

"Look," he said urgently a moment later.

"What? What is it?" Polly had wandered away and was leaning over the balustrades, but she turned and ran back across the terrace to join him.

"This one is loose," he said excitedly. "It's covering one of the doors… Look Polly … it's open, we can get in!"

"Oh, Jeremy. Do you think we should?" gasped Polly. "What if someone catches us?"

"We'll simply say we've come to give a message to Philippe and Hélène," he said, easing the wooden shutter open even further, then pushing the door and squeezing his way through.

The room behind the shutters was ghostly in the dim light. Thin beams of sunlight filtered through the shutters, highlighting the dust as it hung thickly in the air or swirled in the sudden slight breeze from the open door.

They gazed around them in astonishment. The room was almost empty with just a few large objects, presumably furniture, shrouded in dust sheets. Single dusty light bulbs hung from the ceilings where those magnificent crystal chandeliers had been and even the walls were bare, with huge darkened patches where the pictures and tapestries had hung.

All that was the same were the marble columns, and the faces, the de Melville crests which grinned down at them from the mantelpiece and from the mouldings around the doorways and the window frames.

"It doesn't look like the same room," said Jeremy and his voice echoed as if he spoke in a void. "I can't believe all those people were here last night. How could they have packed it all up so quickly?"

"I want to see the other room," said Polly suddenly. "The room where we were waiting."

Jeremy looked around then nodded towards an archway on the far side. "I think it was through there," he said.

He was right. Beyond the archway they found the smaller room.

"Yes," said Polly. "This is it." Turning sharply she looked at Jeremy. "They were here, weren't they?" she said. "We didn't dream it?"

Jeremy didn't answer immediately, just stared around the room, and for the moment it was as if they were there with them again, that if he really concentrated he would see them; Philippe tall and fair, serious looking and older than his years, and Hélène, doll-like Hélène, dancing and laughing with that high-pitched silvery laugh, tossing her head as she beckoned them on.

"No," Jeremy spoke at last, breaking the spell, "we didn't dream it. They were here – but they've gone now. We can only hope my French was good enough. That they understood what I meant and were able to persuade their father to take them somewhere else for their holidays."

"Perhaps they'll be at the same caravan site as us," said Polly hopefully. "Wouldn't that be wonderful, Jeremy?"

"Yes, it would," he agreed. Somehow he doubted that would happen and by now he was even beginning to think they would never see their new friends again. "I think," he said at last, "we should go now."

"Yes," she sighed, "I suppose you're right."

Together they walked back through the silent, shrouded rooms and slipped through the gap in the shutters into the warm bright sunshine on the terrace.

A plane droned overhead, a blackbird sang in the gardens and in the distance they could hear the hum of traffic. Ordinary, everyday sounds that to Jeremy, in an odd sort of way, seemed very comforting.

He secured the shutters as best he could, then they left the terrace, skirted the walls of the château, and moments later they were running back down the drive to the little door in the wall.

Chapter 7

When they reached the farmhouse it was to find their mother up and dressed and sitting in the shade of a tree.

"Are you feeling better?" asked Jeremy while Polly sat on the grass and rested her head against her mother's knee.

"Still a bit fragile, but better than I was," said Mum. Her face looked very pale beneath the brim of her straw sun hat and there were dark smudges around her eyes.

"Where's Dad?" asked Jeremy, looking around.

"He's gone up to the farmhouse to tell the farmer that we shall be moving on tomorrow," said Mum, then before Jeremy had a chance to say anything further, she went on, "Dad was telling me about your friends up at the château – did you see them again?"

It was Polly who answered. "No," she said glumly, looking up at her mother. "They'd gone."

"Oh, that's a shame," said Mum. "Let's hope they haven't gone to Marseilles – Dad was saying the fires around there are pretty bad this morning."

"We know," said Polly. "That's what we went back to tell them."

"I gather you saw inside the château as well," said Mum. "Lucky old things. I would have loved to have been able to go inside." She paused. "What was it like?" she asked and when neither Jeremy nor Polly answered she looked from one to the other. "Was it really super?"

"Yes," Jeremy nodded. "Really super," he said slowly. Suddenly he didn't feel he wanted to explain how different it had been this morning from the night before.

"All columns and things," said Polly. "Oh, and the face, you know, Mum?" She looked quickly at her mother again and when she nodded, she rushed on, "well it was every-where, on the walls, the ceilings, mantel-pieces, window frames … everywhere, wasn't it, Jeremy?" She threw Jeremy a quick look, almost fearful, as if she was afraid she may have said too much.

"Yes," he agreed grimly, "it was."

Mum frowned, then looking up she shaded her eyes with her hand. "Here comes Dad now." As their father crossed the yard to join them she said, "Did you see the farmer, Mike?"

Dad nodded. "Yes," he said. "I told him we'd be away first thing in the morning." He glanced at Polly and Jeremy. "I thought you two might be back," he said.

"Why?" asked Jeremy.

"Something the farmer said," said Dad with a shrug. "You didn't find your friends, did you?" he added after a moment.

Polly threw Jeremy a quick glance. "No," he said at last, "we didn't, but how did you…?"

"How did I know that?" asked Dad. "Well, according to the farmer no one lives at the château any more – it's been empty for at least the last ten years."

Suddenly Jeremy felt as if the world tilted slightly, throwing him horribly off balance, then as it righted itself, he heard his father say, "Those children you met must have been from the town."

"They said their name was de Melville," said Jeremy quietly.

"I guess that was just wishful thinking," said Dad with a laugh. "The only remaining member of the de Melville family, the present Marquis, apparently lives in Paris these days. He is a very elderly man. The farmer said he used to open the château to the public on certain occasions, but like I said, for the last ten years it's been boarded up."

"Well, it wasn't boarded up last night," said Polly. "We know, cos we went in."

"They must have opened it for the pageant," said Mum.

Dad shrugged. "The farmer said not."

"He doesn't know," retorted Polly hotly. "He wasn't there, was he, Jeremy?"

Jeremy shook his head. He still felt rather strange but couldn't really say why.

"Well, never mind," said Mum soothingly,

"it's not worth worrying about. What we have to do now is look forward to the rest of our holiday. We don't seem to have got off to a very good start, but maybe from now on things will be better."

While Mum and Dad were clearing up the last of the rubbish the following morning, for some inexplicable reason Jeremy found himself drawn to the ivy-covered wall. Even as he stood looking at the spot, willing himself to part the ivy, he found Polly beside him.

"What are you doing?" she whispered.

"Don't know really," Jeremy admitted. "I don't like the face, but I felt I should have one last look at it before we go."

"I know what you mean," admitted Polly, then when Jeremy still made no attempt to move she reached up on tip-toe and gingerly parted the leaves.

The orange face grinned down at them.

Jeremy forced himself to look. It was only a clay face, after all. It couldn't possibly harm them.

"We did see them, didn't we?" whispered

Polly as they stared up at the face. "They were there in the labyrinth, and inside the château, weren't they, Jeremy?"

"Yes, they were," said Jeremy.

"Who do you think they were?"

"I don't know," Jeremy admitted. "They said they were de Melvilles but Mum and Dad said they must have been from the town taking part in the pageant, only pretending to be de Melvilles ... and I suppose that would make sense really, especially if the only member of the family is that old man who lives in Paris..."

"Well, I think they were de Melvilles," said Polly stubbornly. "But..." she hesitated, "there were some strange things, weren't there, Jeremy?"

"There certainly were," he agreed. "That storm for one and the way time seemed to stand still..."

"I know," breathed Polly, allowing the leaves to fall back, covering the face again, "and the way the château looked so different. I've been thinking, Jeremy, did you see those weeds in the drive, they were so tall ... as if they'd been growing there for ... for..."

"Ten years?" said Jeremy.

"Well, yes, ten years," said Polly. "But they couldn't have been there for ten years. That carriage the night before … it would have flattened the weeds, wouldn't it?"

"Yes, it would." Jeremy nodded. "And there were other things; that door in the wall, the rust on the handle, the rubbish behind it – it was as if it hadn't been opened for a very long time, and yet we know we opened it only the night before…"

"And the dust in the château – it was thick," Polly went on when Jeremy paused for breath, "and only the night before, all those people were there… It simply doesn't make sense."

Together they turned away from the face on the wall and began walking slowly across the yard to join their parents.

"I don't know what the answer is, Polly," said Jeremy. "I just know some very strange things have happened since we've been here. Maybe we'll never know the answers."

"Come on, you two," called Dad. "I want to get away now."

They climbed into the car and fastened their seat belts.

"What were you doing?" asked Mum from the front seat.

Jeremy suddenly found himself unable to speak and had to leave Polly to answer.

"We were just having a last look at the face on the wall," said Polly.

Mum was silent for a moment, then as they drove out of the farm yard on to the dirt track she looked over her shoulder towards the wall and the ivy that hid its secret so well. "When we get home," she said, "I'll take you to see the house that I knew when I was a child, then you can see the other face for yourselves."

Jeremy wasn't sure he wanted to see it, he'd had enough trouble with this face, and all those others up at the château, but he didn't like to say so.

They were all silent as they drove past the château. The chains were still on the gates while all they could see of the building itself were the glimpses through the trees of the turrets and chimneys.

"I still would like to have seen inside," said Mum.

Dad stayed silent and Jeremy had the distinct impression that he thought they'd made the whole thing up. It gave him a sort of desperate feeling as if he wanted to make his father believe them but something told him it would be useless saying any more.

He glanced at Polly on the seat beside him. Polly knew, and really that was all that mattered. Usually Polly irritated him, but the events of the last two days seemed to have made them closer, better friends, and as they left the château behind them Jeremy decided it would be best if they could try and put the whole thing out of their minds and enjoy what was left of their holiday.

Chapter 8

"Now," said Mum, "the house is somewhere along here on the left." She slowed the car, peering through the windscreen as she spoke.

They had been home from holiday for nearly a week and it had been Polly who had pestered and pestered for Mum to take them to the village where she had lived as a child. Jeremy had very mixed feelings about the whole thing. Part of him desperately wanted to see the face, just to see if it really was the same, but another part, equally as strong, dreaded the very idea.

He had enjoyed the holiday once it had finally got going, even the swimming and the games of cricket on the beach, but the events of those first few days hadn't really been far from his mind in spite of his intentions to forget them.

He had even dreamt of them: the fields of sunflowers, the dark coolness of the labyrinth, Philippe on the steps of the folly, Hélène hiding amongst the trees, the château itself – a blaze of lights, or derelict and forlorn – but throughout it all, the one image that over-shadowed all others was that of the face; the orange, grinning face. It seemed to haunt him, his dreams and his waking moments, as if it was trying to tell him something.

"There it is!" There was no disguising the excitement in his mother's voice as she drew the car into the kerb and switched off the engine.

"And look," she added triumphantly, "there's the face – just as I remembered it."

Jeremy's heart had started that terrible pounding again but he forced himself to look.

The house was white with a roof made of the sort of curved pink tiles you see on houses in France. There were exotic-looking trees and plants in the front garden as well but Jeremy was hardly aware of any of this. All he could think was that there, on the wall between the front door and a window was the face, the same face that he had come to know so well.

Polly had unclipped her seat belt and was scrambling out of the car. His mother also had opened her door.

Why, thought Jeremy desperately, did they need a closer look? Surely they could see all they needed to see from where they were?

"Come on, Jeremy," called Polly over her shoulder, "let's go and see."

"You can't go in there," muttered Jeremy as he joined them on the pavement, "someone lives there."

"I can't believe it's the same lady who lived there when I was a child," said Mum thoughtfully as she leaned over the wall for a better look. "She was old then, at least she seemed old to us children."

"And mad," said Polly solemnly. "You said she was mad."

"Yes, I know I did," agreed Mum. "That's what we thought at the time, but it was probably only that we didn't understand her – that's why we thought she was mad. Dreadful really, when you think about it now," she added, almost to herself.

"It's the same face, isn't it?" said Polly, resting her elbows on the top of the wall and propping up her chin in her hands.

"Yes," said Jeremy grimly, "it certainly is."

"You don't sound very pleased about it," said Mum curiously. "Why's that?"

"I don't know really." Jeremy shrugged, trying to drag his gaze away from the face and failing miserably.

"Can I help you?" said a voice behind them.

They all three swung round to find that while they had been so engrossed in looking at the face a woman on a bicycle had come silently up behind them. Even as they stared at her, she dismounted and pushed the bicycle on to the grass verge.

It was an old, black bicycle Jeremy noticed, with upright handlebars and a wicker basket in front.

112

"Oh, I'm very sorry," said Mum, "do you live here?" She half turned to the house.

The young woman nodded. "Yes, I do." She had a nice face, round and smiling, brown eyes and long hair pushed back from her face with a red band.

"You must think us awfully rude," said Mum. "But we came to look at the face on the wall of your house."

The woman laughed. "Don't worry," she said, "everyone stops to look at that."

"I used to live around here when I was a child," said Mum. "I passed this house on my way to school. The face always fascinated me. There was a lady who lived here then … I believe she was French."

The woman nodded again. "She was the previous owner of the house," she said. "And yes, she was French. Her name was Madame de Melville. Her late husband apparently was a member of the French aristocracy. The face is their family crest."

"We know," said Polly excitedly. "We've just been to France on holiday. We saw the château where the de Melvilles lived…" She trailed off as Jeremy dug her in the ribs with his elbow.

Suddenly he was afraid at how much she was going to say. He couldn't imagine trying to explain everything to this woman, nice as she seemed, who after all, was a stranger. And let's face it, he thought, if they did try to tell her what had happened she would, no doubt, think they were the ones who were mad.

"Do you know anything else about the family?" asked Mum.

The woman smiled and shook her head. "No, sorry," she said. "My husband wanted to take the face down, he doesn't like it for some reason…"

Don't blame him, thought Jeremy.

"…but I persuaded him to leave it there. It certainly provides a talking point."

Mum agreed and thanked her for letting them look, then as the woman opened the gate and wheeled her bicycle inside they climbed back into the car.

"Well, that's that." Mum rested her hands on the steering wheel for a moment as they all took one last look at the house. "At least we know now that it was the same face and what the connection was."

"I wish the other lady had still been there," said Polly with a pout.

"I didn't really think she could still be alive." Mum switched on the engine and put the car into gear.

"What's arist … aristoc…?" asked Polly as they drove away.

"Aristocracy?" Mum finished the word for her. "It means the nobility."

"Like the Royal Family?" asked Polly.

"Sort of," said Mum.

Jeremy sighed as they turned out of the tree-lined road and left the house behind. It was true the connection between the faces had now been established but it hadn't really told them any more or helped to explain those strange events they had experienced in France.

He had just reached the conclusion that probably nothing would ever give him the explanation he wanted when they reached home, only to find Dad waiting for them with a book he'd just found in the local library.

"I knew you'd be interested in this," he said, opening the book and turning the pages. "It's an illustrated history of the French nobility, most of whom lost their lives during the French Revolution – and there's a section on the de Melville family."

Jeremy swallowed and stared at the book. It was a very ordinary sort of book, large and thick, with a dark green cover, but as his father began speaking again Jeremy felt as if his legs were slowly turning to jelly.

"It says the de Melville family home was a large château near the city of Toulouse," said Dad. "And look, there's a picture."

"Our château," breathed Polly as they all gazed down at a colour photograph of the pink stone château with its grey shutters.

"They even have a picture of the family crest," Dad went on, turning the page.

The face grinned up at them.

Jeremy shuddered, then forced himself to concentrate as Dad flicked the pages again and carried on talking.

"Like I said, most members of the aristocracy at the time lost their heads but –

and here's the fascinating part – apparently the Marquis de Melville and his wife and children were set to make their escape from the French port of Marseilles, when –" Dad paused and turned the page – "according to this, family legend has it that they received a warning or some sort of tip-off, and in consequence, at the eleventh hour they changed their plans and fled to Bordeaux. From there they later made their way to a small port in the north of France and escaped to England in a fishing vessel. Their friends and other relatives who had gathered at their château near Toulouse chose not to heed the warning and carried on to Marseilles where the revolutionaries were waiting for them."

"What happened to them?" whispered Polly, her eyes huge.

"They were taken to Paris where, I'm afraid, they met their fate," said Dad grimly.

"Oh dear," said Mum.

"However," Dad went on more cheerfully, "our family from the château were quite safe, and it says here, that to commemorate their good fortune a pageant is re-enacted in the grounds of their château each year by local townsfolk."

"That's what you two must have seen," said Mum, looking at Jeremy and Polly. "Does it say who warned the de Melvilles, Mike?" she added.

"I don't think so…" Dad began perusing the pages again, then shook his head. "No," he concluded at last. "It must have been someone who knew the movements of the revolutionaries but who sympathized with the family. Maybe they were good landlords and the locals respected them."

He turned the last page.

"Oh," he said, "here is another picture – it's a portrait of the family. The Marquis and Marquise de Melville and their two children." He turned the book so that Jeremy and Polly could see.

The Marquis was standing near the fountains in the gardens of the château, his wife seated before him on the low stone wall. And by their sides, looking exactly as they had done before, were Philippe, in his purple satin shirt and grey breeches and Hélène in her blue dress.

It was dim and cool in the shed at the bottom of the garden. It was a very large shed and the bench at the far end that ran along the entire wall belonged to Jeremy. This was where he carried out his inventions – the inventions that he had hoped would one day leave their mark in history.

He stood for a long time staring at the bench but without really seeing all the paraphernalia that littered the top – the bits of metal, the iron filings, lengths of string and scraps of paper covered with formulae and designs.

He didn't know how long he stood there but it was a faint scratching noise on the door that finally brought him to. When he opened the door he found Polly outside – a wide-eyed, rather fearful-looking Polly.

"Come in," he said, opening the door wider then closing it behind her. They sat down on a couple of canvas garden chairs and stared at one another.

"What happened?" asked Polly at last. "Whatever was it all about?"

"I'm still trying to work it out," said Jeremy.

"It was them, wasn't it?" Polly's voice was little more than a whisper. "In the book, the portrait, it was them."

"Yes," said Jeremy, "it was them. No doubt about that."

"Were they ghosts?" asked Polly. She said it quickly as if she had to ask the question, get the words out, before she changed her mind.

"No." Jeremy shook his head. "They were too real to be ghosts."

Polly frowned. "So were we the ghosts then?"

"We couldn't have been," Jeremy replied slowly. "To be a ghost you have to have died. That was the eighteenth century – we hadn't been born then."

"But we were there," cried Polly. "And if they were real…"

"They were real," said Jeremy firmly. "So when you really think about it, that leaves only one possible explanation."

"What?" breathed Polly, her eyes growing enormous.

"Dad said the family legend was that they received a warning not to go to Marseilles," said Jeremy. He stopped, his eyes shining with excitement, then he said, "We were the ones who warned them."

"I still don't understand," wailed Polly.

"Don't you see," said Jeremy urgently. "We had a mission, although we didn't know it at the time. Our mission was to travel back through time to the eighteenth century to deliver the warning to the de Melville family – and we did it, Polly. We really did it."

"Wow!" said Polly.

"And when you really think about that, it explains it all," said Jeremy. "We were in the present at the pageant, those people there were just acting out the past, but when we entered the labyrinth that was when we stepped back into the past. We met Philippe and Hélène, we warned them not to go to Marseilles…"

"But wasn't that because of the forest fires?" Polly looked bewildered.

"That was the present danger – the one we understood." Jeremy was beginning to grow excited as all the pieces began to fall into place. "But don't you see," he hurried on, "the warning was simply of danger in Marseilles, but it applied both to the present – the fire – and to the past – the revolutionaries. We warned them not to go. My French wasn't really good enough to explain why they shouldn't go, simply that they would be in danger if they did. They must have told their parents, who may have even suspected there was danger there, I don't know. But obviously it was enough to decide them."

"So when did we get back into the present?" Polly still looked bewildered.

"I'm not sure." Jeremy screwed up his face trying to remember. "I think," he went on at last, "I think it must have been when we got outside the château – yes, that's it, when we got back to the road – do you remember that car that passed us?"

Polly nodded. "Yes," she said excitedly. "They didn't have cars then did they, Jeremy?"

"No," he said, "they had horse-drawn carriages."

"Oh!" Polly gasped, covering her mouth with her hands.

"It explains it all," Jeremy rushed on, "the storm, why we were wet one minute and not the next – why time stood still –"

"And the château," Polly chipped in, "why it was full of furniture and paintings and things that night, and why only the next morning it was empty, and dusty, and shut up."

"Exactly," said Jeremy triumphantly. "Because it wasn't the next morning, it was about two hundred years later. And there's another thing," he rushed on excitedly. "All those people that were there that night. We thought it was a party at the time, but now I don't think it was anything of the sort. I think those were the de Melvilles' friends and relatives who had gathered at the château ready to escape to Marseilles, just like it said in the book, only they were the ones who didn't heed the warning. They carried on to Marseilles where the revolutionaries were waiting for them ... they were taken to Paris..."

"Where they lost their heads..." Solemnly, Polly finished the sentence.

They remained quiet for a long time, then it was Polly who broke the silence. "Do you think," she said, "that Mum and Dad know?"

"Not a chance." Jeremy shook his head. "They think we were simply involved in the pageant."

"And what about the face? Was that anything to do with it?"

Jeremy threw her a sharp glance. He still didn't really want Polly knowing how disturbed he'd been by the face.

"I think it was part of it," he said slowly at last, "maybe a sort of warning to us that something was going to happen. I don't know…"

"So what do you think would have happened if we hadn't gone to France?" asked Polly a moment later. "If we hadn't gone to the château or met Philippe and Hélène?"

"I don't think there was a chance of us not going," Jeremy replied slowly. "I think it had all been planned – the cancelled trip to Marseilles, and us ending up at the farm, then at the craft fair."

He paused and Polly stared at him. "Because if we hadn't," he continued after a moment, "the family would have been killed – the de Melvilles would have been wiped out. As it was, they escaped to England."

"What about the old man living in Paris?" asked Polly.

Jeremy shrugged. "I guess some of them returned to France after the revolution."

"And the old French woman who used to live in the house we saw today?"

"She was married to a de Melville," Jeremy replied thoughtfully. "He must have been a descendent, like the old man in Paris. I really don't know, Polly, but whichever way you look at things, it seems like we have been responsible for preventing a tragedy that would have happened all those years ago."

"Wow," said Polly again. Then after a moment, she added, "You always did want to do something important, didn't you Jeremy? Well, I guess there aren't many things more important than saving people's lives." She fell silent again, then wistfully she said, "The only thing is – we won't ever see them again, will we?"

"I shouldn't think so," said Jeremy.

"I wish we could. I really liked them. They were so different from our other friends."

"They certainly were," Jeremy agreed. "But…" he paused.

"Yes?" said Polly eagerly.

"You never know," he said darkly. "We've travelled back once to help them. Maybe it'll happen again one day."

"Oh yes," breathed Polly. "Maybe it will."